Little Grey Rabbit

WATER RAT'S PICNIC

Little Grey Rabbit

WATER RAT'S PICNIC

By Alison Uttley
Pictures by Margaret Tempest

templar
books

One day Water Rat strolled down towards his boathouse. There lay the Saucy Nancy, the prettiest little boat you ever saw.

"Where are you going today?" asked his housekeeper, Mrs Webster.

"I'm going to invite some friends on a water-picnic," said Water Rat. "They've never seen a boat before."

Water Rat paddled upstream. At the water's edge a waterhen was busy washing.

"Watch out for the ducks today," she called. "They're being very tiresome."

Water Rat thanked her, moored his boat and walked across the fields to Little Grey Rabbit's house.

Grey Rabbit was carefully ladling jam into jars.

"I came to invite you and Squirrel on a boat-picnic," said Water Rat.

"A real live boat?" said Squirrel excitedly.

"A real live picnic?" shouted Hare from outside.

"I'm afraid my boat only holds three," said Water Rat. "But suppose you race along the river bank, Hare, while I row the others? Then you can choose the place for the picnic."

"That's a good idea," said Hare, and it was settled.

They locked the door and tripped along by Water Rat's side, asking about the boat.

Down at the river, Hare waved goodbye. "Take care of the food and don't fall in," he called, then he galloped out of sight.

Water Rat rowed with graceful sweeps, past a green frog and buttercups and the waterhen's fourteen chicks.

Suddenly there was
a flurry as a flock of
white ducks came
hurrying up.

"Don't shake the
boat!" said Water Rat.

But one duck
snatched Squirrel's
sunshade and another
took Grey Rabbit's
apron.

There was such a commotion that nobody noticed
another duck seize the picnic basket.

"Oh! Oh!!" cried Grey Rabbit and Squirrel.

The duck tried to open the basket but it slipped and sank down, down to the bottom of the river.

Water Rat took off his velvet coat and dived overboard. He hauled the basket into the boat and clambered in after it. But the apron and the sunshade were lost.

Water Rat picked a lily leaf to replace Squirrel's sunshade, and they rowed away from the ducks to look for Hare.

When Hare heard the picnic was nearly lost he clasped it to his heart.

"That would have been a calamity!" he exclaimed.

Back on shore, Grey Rabbit and Squirrel picked up sticks, Water Rat filled the kettle and Hare lit a crackling fire.

Then Hare leapt for joy when he saw the sandwiches in their waterproof wrappers. What a feast there was!

As the others washed their cups at the river's edge, Hare crept softly out of sight.

"You didn't know I could row," he called, splashing.

"Oh Hare, take care!" shrieked Squirrel.

The oars waved wildly, Hare's feet flew up, and he shot backwards into the water.

"Save me!" he cried. "I'm drowning!"

Out of the shadows came the ducks, one with the blue apron over her shoulders, another with the red sunshade.

The ducks grabbed Hare and swam to shore with him. Then away they went, cackling with laughter.

Squirrel and Grey Rabbit dried him with their handkerchiefs and Water Rat swam after the little boat.

"I'm going home," said Hare crossly and he trotted off with his head bent.

"Would you like to see my house?" said
Water Rat to the others. "It's quite near."

Grey Rabbit and Squirrel were delighted.
In the hall stood an aquarium full of
weeds and fish. Squirrel could hardly tear
herself away from it, but Water Rat led
them to the parlour.

There Mrs Webster brought out some water-lily jam and Water Rat gave the guests a bag of watercress.

"We should go home," said Grey Rabbit. "Poor Hare is waiting for us."

"Thank you, Water Rat," called Squirrel and Grey Rabbit, and they scampered home.

A violent sneeze shook the house as they came in. Squirrel and Grey Rabbit raced upstairs and soon Hare was snug in bed with a pot of elderflower tea.

As they walked downstairs they heard footsteps flipping to the door, then quietly flipping away.

Little Grey Rabbit stepped outside to look. There was her blue apron, very wet. But the sunshade never came back. Any day now you can still see the ducks swimming on the river, carrying Squirrel's sunshade…

THE END